For Zuey, Arjun, and Leykh —S.K.

To my Ammumma —P.P.

STERLING CHILDREN'S BOOKS
New York

An Imprint of Sterling Publishing Co., Inc.
122 Fifth Avenue
New York, NY 10011

Text © 2021 Supriya Kelkar
Illustrations © 2021 Parvati Pillai

ISBN 978-1-4549-4020-3

Distributed in Canada by Sterling Publishing Co., Inc.
c/o Canadian Manda Group, 664 Annette Street
Toronto, Ontario M6S 2C8, Canada
Distributed in the United Kingdom by GMC Distribution Services
Castle Place, 166 High Street, Lewes, East Sussex BN7 1XU, England
Distributed in Australia by NewSouth Books
University of New South Wales, Sydney, NSW 2052, Australia

For information about custom editions, special sales, and premium and corporate purchases,
please contact Sterling Special Sales at 800-805-5489 or specialsales@sterlingpublishing.com.

Manufactured in China

Lot#
2 4 6 8 10 9 7 5 3 1
12/20

sterlingpublishing.com

Interior and cover design by Irene Vandervoort and Jo Obarowski
The artwork in this book was created digitally.

BINDU'S BINDIS

BY

SUPRIYA KELKAR

ILLUSTRATED BY

PARVATI PILLAI

STERLING CHILDREN'S BOOKS
New York

Every month **BINDU'S** nani sent her
a new set of bindis from India.

Bindu adored her bindis.

She wore them to
the **temple**.

She wore them on
holidays.

She wore them at
home.

Packet upon packet. Shape after shape.
The choices were endless.

Lightning bolts were perfect for a **brave** day.

Ovals were just the thing for a **proud** performance.

And squiggly lines practically shouted,

"I'm **unique**!"

One month, Nani brought the bindis in person.

Bindu was so excited, she wore a brilliant oval bindi. She couldn't wait to see what Nani had on.

But on the way back from the airport, Bindu suddenly wasn't feeling excited anymore.

She wanted to slip her bindi off.
She wanted to go home.

Bindu watched Nani drum her fingers. She looked
even more worried than Bindu. . . .

So Bindu squeezed her hand.

When the murmurs outside got louder, Bindu talked
over them, so neither she nor Nani could hear them.

And when Bindu and Nani felt the stares, Bindu held
her head up high. And Nani did the same.

After all, they loved to match!

That evening, Nani drank chai and told stories of dancing in the rain back home for all the world to see.

She even showed Bindu some new (old) moves.

Every day after school, Bindu would come home and
pick out a bindi to match Nani.

A **flower** on the forehead was just right for silly giggles.

Diamonds twinkled with an adventurous wink.

And **circles** did the trick for a festive feeling.

Soon the time came for Bindu to wear her **lightning bolt** bindi to school.

It was Bindu's first time wearing one there,
so Nani made sure she matched her.

But when it was Bindu's turn on stage, she suddenly wasn't feeling very brave.

She wanted to slip her bindi off.
She wanted to go home.

Do you want to wear **circles**?

"No," Bindu replied.

"How about **ovals**?"

Bindu shook her head.

"**Squiggly lines**?" asked Nani.
"I'm sick of feeling unique," said Bindu,
refusing to move as her music started.

Bindu looked nervous.
So, Nani squeezed her hand . . .

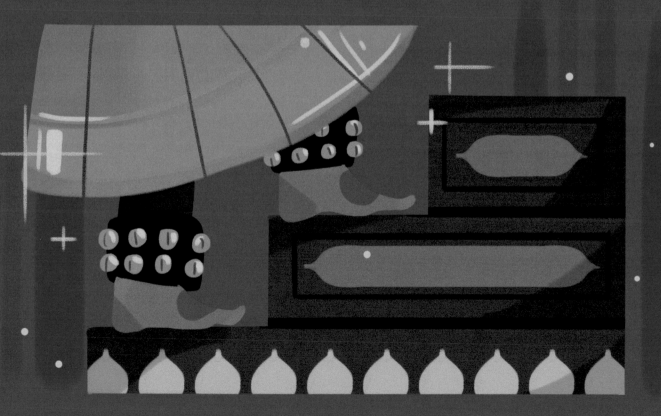

. . . and got up on stage.

Nani began to twirl.
Some people stared. Nani almost stopped . . .
but Bindu held her head up high, so Nani did the same.

Nani shook her hips.
Some people murmured.
So Bindu cheered over them,
swaying along to the music in her seat.

And soon everyone
began to cheer.

Bindu neared the stage. She watched as the lights
made Nani's bindi sparkle until she couldn't tell

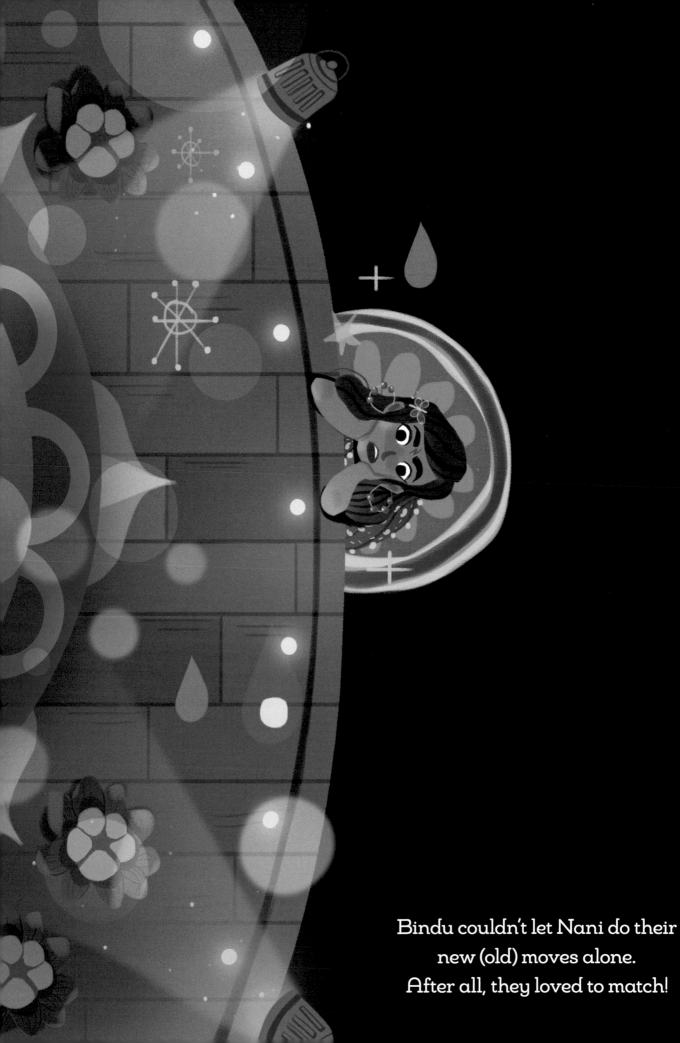

Bindu couldn't let Nani do their
new (old) moves alone.
After all, they loved to match!

So Bindu bravely got up on stage with Nani . . .

twirled with Nani . . .

and shook her hips with Nani.

Because Bindu
adored her bindis . . .

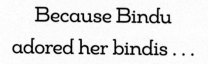

she wore them to the
temple . . .

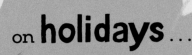

on **holidays**...

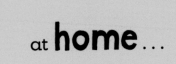

at **home**...

and she wore them for dancing with her Nani. For all the world to see.

BINDIS

Bindis are worn in parts of Asia and its diaspora by some members of the community.

In South Asia and the South Asian diaspora, some people wear bindis daily, and some wear them only when dressing up or for holidays or religious ceremonies. Some people wear them out of custom or for religious purposes. In Hinduism, bindis are worn to activate the area associated with the third eye. While a bindi can have a religious meaning, it is also worn cosmetically or because of tradition in the South Asian community by people from many religions.

"Bindi" is a Hindi and Punjabi word. The bindi has many different names in other Indian languages and sometimes multiple names in the same language, including "tikkli" or "kunku" in Marathi, "tillo" in Konkani, "pottu" in Malyalam, "bottu" in Telugu, "chandlo" in Gujarati, "kumkuma," in Kannada, and "teep" in Bengali. And these are just a few of the names for a bindi in just a few of the languages spoken in the South Asian diaspora.

Bindis traditionally are made of vermilion powder that can be applied by fingertip to make a circle. Bindis can also be in a liquid form, applied by a small-tipped brush. Today, bindis are commonly available as a set, in little packets, like Nani sends Bindu. They come with an adhesive backing so you can easily stick them on and reuse them. Bindis come in all sorts of shapes and colors, including all the shapes Bindu wears in this story.